Toothbrush, Jammies, Man in the Moon . . .

WHY IS IT BEDTIME SO SOON?

By Nicole Tocco

MODERN PUBLISHING
A DIVISION OF
UNISYSTEMS, INC.

New York, New York

Text and Art Copyright ©2006 Modern Publishing, a division of Unisystems, Inc.
All Rights Reserved.

Based on a title created by Wendy Rosen
Illustrated by ⓠ Creative Quotient

Published by Modern Publishing, a division of Unisystems, Inc. No part of this book may
be reproduced, stored in a retrieval system, or transmitted in any form without written
permission from the publisher.

Modern Publishing
A Division of Unisystems, Inc.
New York, New York
Printed in the U.S.A.
Modernpublishing.com

2 4 6 8 10 9 7 5 3
Library of Congress Cataloging-in-Publication Data
Tocco, Nicole.
Toothbrush, jammies, man in the moon-- why is it bedtime so soon?/
by Nicole Tocco.
p. cm.
Summary: A little girl prepares for bed, all the while protesting that
she is not sleepy.
ISBN-13: 978-0-7666-2463-4
[1. Bedtime--Fiction. 2. Stories in rhyme.]   I. Title.
PZ8.3.T556To 2006
[E]--dc22
2006019200

For Grandpa

Every night,
no matter what,
I hear the words
I dread.

Mom and Dad call out to us,
"Let's go, it's time for bed!"

I'm just not tired. I'm wide awake.
So what if the moon is bright?

I don't understand. It's just not fair!
WHY can't I stay up all night?

Mom and Dad have a good reason why I need lots of rest.

"If you don't get a good night's sleep,
you won't be at your best!"

But I'm just not
ready for bed.
I still have so
much to do!

Like color a picture...

...and read a book...

...and play a fun game, too!

Dad says, "Bedtime's as fun as playtime.
So, come on and grab your bear Freddy!"

Mom says, "I bet you'll be so, so sleepy once you're all done getting ready!"

I'm wearing mud from my soccer game,
Some finger paints, and even my dessert!

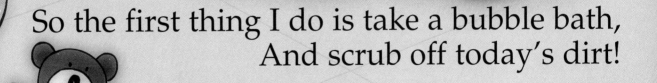

So the first thing I do is take a bubble bath,
And scrub off today's dirt!

After I step out of the tub,
Mommy combs my hair.

I put on a fluffy robe,
And so does my bear!

Now it's time to brush my teeth,
To make them clean and bright.

So I step up on my stool
Till I can reach just right!

My pajamas are so comfy.
They're my favorite thing to wear!

They keep me very cozy.
This is my favorite pair!

I feel thirsty before bedtime.
I almost always do!

Daddy gives me
a little drink
So I can sleep
the whole night through!

I have to make
a pit stop,
And go potty
just once more!

I do that each and every night
Before I start to snore!

It's time to hop into my bed,
and snuggle under the sheets.

Mommy and Daddy tuck me in,
So I'm snug from head to feet!

Now it's time for a story!
I pick out my very best book.
Daddy reads it to me
While Freddy takes a look!

I think about all of the things
That I am so thankful for.
I count all of my blessings
And wish for many more!

Next it's time for
a good-night kiss
And a big, sweet
good-night hug!

You know what?
I'm very tired.
Now that I'm clean
and warm and snug!

Before I know it, I'm asleep.
Soon I'll have sweet dreams.

My turn for bedtime!

Mom and Dad were right after all—
Bedtime's not as bad as it seems!